Walter J. Raymond

Horrors of the Modern Deluge!

Descriptive and illustrated review of the great floods of the Mississippi

and Ohio rivers

Walter J. Raymond

Horrors of the Modern Deluge!
Descriptive and illustrated review of the great floods of the Mississippi and Ohio rivers

ISBN/EAN: 9783337239008

Printed in Europe, USA, Canada, Australia, Japan

Cover: Foto ©Andreas Hilbeck / pixelio.de

More available books at **www.hansebooks.com**

HORRORS

—OF THE—

MODERN DELUGE!

DESCRIPTIVE AND ILLUSTRATED REVIEW

—OF THE—

GREAT FLOODS

—OF THE—

MISSISSIPPI AND OHIO RIVERS,

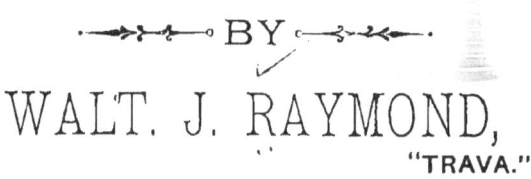

WALT. J. RAYMOND,

"TRAVA."

1882.

PREFATORY.

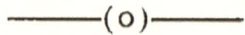

The ensuing pages illustrate the horrors of the greatest deluge the history of the world records since the Christian era.

Over seventy-five thousand square miles of a fertile and productive country have been devastated and laid waste by the relentless waters.

The illustrations are from the pencil of Mr. A. B. Greene, St. Louis' well known artist, who accompanied the Expedition during its entire trip.

The reports herein published were prepared by Mr. Walt. J. Raymond (Trava), who visited the inundated country and witnessed the scenes as herein related. Being a graphic and forcible writer, this history of the

MODERN DELUGE

· will be the most consecutive and interesting published.

A. E. GOTTSCHALK & CO.,

PUBLISHERS.

THE MODERN DELUGE.

CHAPTER I.

The history of the world records but one Deluge.

The history of the world, as it advances, will record that, in the time between January 21st and April 1st, 1882, an unconquerable deluge swept over the Western Continent, along the line of the Mississippi River, carrying famine, destruction and death throughout a country over 75,000 square miles in extent.

It will record the fact, that in a night the rushing waters deluged and drowned hundreds of helpless whites and negroes, who inhabited the low level of the Mississippi bottom lands.

It will record the fact, that nearly all animal life throughout a country 800 miles in length, with an average width of 35 miles, was swept from existence.

It will record the fact, that the houseless, naked tenants of those miserable apologies for homes, being driven from the floor to the roofs of their shanties, and from that last refuge to limbs of trees and floating driftwood, were passed by crowded steamers, unable to succor or relieve, and left to rot, in death, beneath the rays of a semi-tropic sun.

Modern history, on this crisis in the every-day life of the Southwestern country, will, among other things, record that the urgent needs from all directions, ranging over so vast a territory, would not admit of stopping private enterprise to attend to individual cases of distress. It will argue that the confusion attendant upon such a calamity to a country, temporally unjointed the philanthropic balance of their natures, and made them blind and deaf to the appealing attitudes, the heart-piercing cries for succor that went up from sloughs, bayous and river bottoms for 800 miles along the Mississippi River.

It will, these modern times, perpetuate in history, through the art preservative and the columns of the press, the heartless effrontery of speculative steamboat lessees, in their announcements that for $4.00 any number of hundreds of the citizens of a given city on the banks of the flooded districts can be treated to a view of the bloated, swollen and decomposing carcasses of man and beast along the line of the proposed trip. That $4.00 per capita will carry a crowd of a thousand over the watery sepulchre, beneath whose dirty, turgid surface possibly can be seen the horrors of that agonizing death which overtook the hundreds and thousands that perished in this, the modern deluge.

Appended to these facts, in the history of the three months taken from the year 1882, will be found, if the chronicler of these times be truthful, delightful descriptions of various trips, each representing enthusiastic crowds engaged in feasting and gorging the innerman with rare viands and costly wines, as they sail the watery grave.

If the field-glasses carried upon the occasion of these trips by beaux and belles could speak, they would recount a tale of horror now locked in the fair and brave breasts of these admiring crowds.

They could, with graphic vividness, depict the ghoul of despair sitting side by side of the shivering human beings, and the livid corpses, which are promiscuously piled together upon nine-tenths of the shanties within five miles of the river's banks. They could tell of a waste of waters in all directions, as far as the eye could reach, surrounding tottering cabins and huts, upon the roofs of which are huddled three, five, and sometimes ten starving wretches, whose emaciated, blanched and shivering bodies are grappling with gaunt famine. They could tell, as they sweep the colorless horizon of this deluge, of floating, half destroyed anatomies of human beings, swollen to bursting, keeping company, in their southward trip with the current, with hogs, mules, cattle, dogs, and every conceivable living creature that had, before the death-knell of this deluge sounded in their ears, peopled the low lands of this fair country; and still they sailed, sailed out onto the muddy bosom of the father of waters, with merry jest and laughter-sparkling eyes.

CHAPTER II.

The Flood, Morning of January 23d.

Clear and warm. Two hundred miles below the junction of the Ohio and Mississippi Rivers, at the little peninsular which forms the extreme southern point of the State of Illinois, and upon which is built the city of Cairo, the morning of January 23d, 1882, broke as peacefully and calm as a New England Sabbath.

The season was well advanced for the date it bore in the new year, and the budding foliage told of an early and thrifty opening of plantation life. The Mississippi River, which strolled by the grassy banks with languid flow, bore upon its bosom the peace of contented waters.

One hundred miles below the junction of these two rivers the same quiet and undisturbed motion of the waters ran calmly by the cane knoll of its boundary.

Fifty miles below the point of this meeting of waters, the swelling tide began to show signs of drift-wood and a hurrying pace.

Twenty-five miles below, and the banks began to feel the rise, while at the point of the meeting of the two rivers it is rising three feet an hour.

The Ohio River, which has its source at the junction of the Alleghany and Monongahela Rivers, at Pittsburgh, Pa,, is pouring a flood of water into the Mississippi at Cairo.

The small tributaries of the Mississippi, and its main artery, the Missouri River, are rising slowly from the effects of the deluging rains, extending over a period of nearly two months, and the melting of the enormous snow fields at the source of the Missouri, and are emptying three million cubic feet of water into the Mississippi River every hour.

Telegraphs are being sent to all important points South, between Cairo and New Orleans.

CAIRO, January 23d, 1882.

" Unprecedented rise of river. Flood expected. Protect your stock."

Such was the tenor of dispatches sent every hour during the first thirty-six hours of the rise. But quicker, if possible, than the electric spark, the mighty torrent of those two rivers met, entirely submerging the lower point of land which marks the terminus of the State of Illinois, and worked its way up the channel gauge to 47 feet 9 inches above low water mark.

It swept everything before it. Cairo was seven-eighths under water one week after the rise began, and the confluence of the two rivers was estimated to be sixty miles wide.

A force of 1,000 men were employed by the Municipality of the city of Cairo to protect the levee along the city line, and no cessation was made in their work night or day for three weeks. All trains were stopped at this point, and communication with the outside world suspended from necessity.

The horrors of the flood began to make themselves felt, as portions of shanties and more pretentious dwellings were seen floating by, on both the Ohio and the Mississippi Rivers, at Cairo. They were heeled over, and bottom side up, with remnants of apparel clinging to their creaking sides. It told a story of surprise and death.

Cattle and hogs began to be seen on the two rivers January 26th; some with life, and struggling to sustain themselves, but more, dead and swollen from long exposure in the water.

The deluge was upon that fair country through which majestically sweeps the greatesf water course of the world. At intervals, for 900 miles down through South land, it tore away the embankments and levees as if made of straw. It swept out and beyond its boundaries until, in many places, it became 100 miles wide. It drowned hundreds of the inhabitants throughout the bottom lands ere they could get from their beds and flee to the highlands.

It hurried to an easy death thousands upon thousands of cattle, sheep and hogs, and entirely annihilated all poultry, rabbits and small game. Deer, bears, Opossums and wild cats were driven from the swamps of Arkansas to the upland, where they were slaughtered by hundreds with clubs and any weapon of death. Mules and horses were stampeded, to be again overtaken and drowned, in droves of hundreds. I saw forty-six dead mules, in one lot, thrown ashore by the receding waters at Blue Points, 100 miles south of Memphis, on March 10th.

The line of destruction and death was marked by flocks of those scavengers   of   Southern soil, the buzzards, as they gorged on the bloated carcasses of man and beast.

CHAPTER III.

THE START.

I leave the city of Cairo February 18, at 12, midnight.

The flood has now been on twenty-four days   There is no abatement in its rise.

With some danger and great difficulty, the special steam tug that is to convey us over the deluged country swings from her moorings at the Cairo Short Line wharf, out into the stream, and is hurried southward. We throw our line, and find the current registers thirteen miles an hour.

The speed is momentarily quickened, until thirty minutes out from Cairo we are making seventeen miles an hour.   In forty-five minutes we can tally nineteen miles, and as we sweep round the bend between Columbus, Kentucky, and Belmont, Missouri, we register twenty-two miles an hour.   We speed between the high bluffs of the Kentucky side, and the long, level stretch marking the present site of Belmont, and hear the roar of the flood as it quickens its depth and force.

The elevator at Belmont stands out grim and spectral, as we are shot by it with a lightning rapidity. I have just time to recall the fact that this water way between the two States was foremost in the war of the Confederacy, as marking the early battle-ground, if not the first in the West, where Gen. Grant attempted to establish a garrison and entrenchment on the Missouri side.   The high bluffs in the hands of the Confederates overlooking the river, and directly facing Belmont, were mounted with 8-35 pound guns. General Grant's command did not stop long in Belmont.

The water has gained the high grounds of both of these landings. A powerful night glass reveals the long, sinuous encroachment of this destroying element, as it wraps around and searches out the buildings, stock, and what animal life may exist in the levels along the bottoms.

Three weeks later I repassed this point in the steamer City of Helena, and the water still surrounded both villages. The damage to property and life must have been something fabulous.

The situation is scarcely grasped ere the hurrying lights along the banks of both landings are mere specks in the horizon, and the broad sweep given the bosom of the Mississippi just below—south of the above locations—spread out before us like a sea.

CHAPTER IV.

COTTONWOOD POINT.

STATION FOR GOVERNMENT SUPPLIES.

This settlement extends along the banks of the river for a distance of about one mile, and contains about 200 inhabitants. At the time of my arrival it was entirely under water. I counted forty dug-outs and canoes centered about a building submerged to its door-sills. Messrs. H. C. Garrett & Co., who conduct the store and post-office, stated that the water had fallen about three inches in the twenty-four hours previous to my arrival. The back country, for a distance of eighteen miles, is from three to ten feet under water, and the cattle ranges are strewn with hundreds of dead carcasses. In many instances they were unable to get their hides. The inhabitants of Cottonwood were out of supplies, and were approaching a condition of destitution of an alarming character until aided by the Government.

The steamer City of Helena took on refugees, cattle and hogs, to be landed up the river on dry ground.

LOUTWELL,

two miles below, was filled with refugees from the back country. Water stood three and four feet deep on the first floors of several buildings I visited, and I was informed by those who were carried north on the steamer that such had been their condition for more than three weeks.

AT HALE'S POINT,

about twenty miles south of the above landing, there were fourteen houses under water, ranging from four to seven feet deep · the roofs of many of the squatters' shanties being on y visible. The river at this point was estimated to be seventy-five miles wide. At

BARSFIELD

it was thought the river was forty-five miles in width.

The beautiful estate, including all the houses, of Mr. Joe Carr, were about three feet under water. Mr. Carr is famous in Southern history for his hospitality and genial manners, and his loss will be deeply regretted.

SHUTE 26,

a cut-off just above Ashelport, was running about fifty feet of water.

Tuesday, March 14, at 3:50 in the afternoon, the steamer City of Helena was hailed by the special steam dispatch boat Safford, of the *Globe-Democrat*, St. Louis, in charge of Mr. Spink, with an able corps of assistants, including Mr. Wm. F. Gore and Wm. A. Hobbs.

Dispatches were received by Capt. Fleming, to be forwarded from Cairo.

Mr. Spink reported no high land between Tipton and Memphis.

The Safford left Cairo Monday night, March 11, and was twenty-two hours out from that point when hailed.

POWELL'S LANDING.

A family of seven, consisting of five women and two men, with twelve head of cattle and three horses, were taken aboard here. No money. They were carried to Saxton and unloaded.

CHAPTER V.

NUMBER OF FAMILIES IN DISTRESS, EXTENDING OVER AN AREA OF 100 MILES. OSCEOLA, MISSISSIPPI COUNTY, ARK., WITHIN A RADIUS OF TEN MILES.

	Families.	Persons.
Belmont, Mississippi County, Missouri, -	60	300
James Bayou, " " " -	10	60
New Madrid, New Madrid Co., Mo. -	150	750
Bosse's Landing, Lake County, Tenn., -	8	40
Ralfort, " " " -	20	125
Hathaway, " " " -	10	70
Yazoo, Pemiscot County, Missouri, -	75	450
Caruthersville, " " " - -	30	266
Booth's Point, Dyer County, Tenn., -	15	75
Cottonwood Point, Pemiscott County, Mo.,	75	450
Hickman, Mississippi " Ark.,	40	200
Ashport, Lauderdale " , Tenn.,	15	80
Hale's Point, " " "	25	75
Barrsfield, Mississippi " Ark.,	15	75
Elmot, " " "	300	1,500

From Tiptonville to Memphis, a distance of 162 miles, the Mississippi River is estimated to be seventy-five miles wide.

Lautwell's Landing, Arkansas.

CHAPTER VI.

THE GOVERNMENT RATIONS AT MEMPHIS SACKED BY WORTHLESS NEGROES INFESTING THE BACK COUNTIES.

The appeal from the States bordering the line of the Mississippi River, south of the Missouri and Illinois boundaries, for aid in the form of rations, clothing and shelter, was magnanimously responded to by the Government, cap italists and merchants. The magnificent steamers which ply these waters were loaded to the guards—under the direction of staff and line officers of the regular army— with coffee, cornmeal, flour, bacon, clothing, tents, etc., and stations for the distribution of these stores were opened at Memphis, Tenn., Little Rock, Ark., and at various points in the States of Louisiana and Mississippi.

It is claimed by many prominent citizens, and also by some portions of the press of Western Tennessee, that the necessities of that State raised by the flood were not of such a character as to seek relief at the hands of the Government. This may be traced to pride—commendable if you please—but a station for the distribution of food, tents and clothing was opened in the city of Memphis, Tenn.

The scene which followed the opening of the doors beggars description.

From all directions the scavengers of southern soil—the worthless darkey—flocked to this point and made clamorous complaints of unheard destitution, and demanded aid.

The officers in charge not familiar with the sneaking, thieving nature of the majority of these colored tramps, were being sadly duped, when reputable citizens and the press of Memphis enlightened the Government's almsgivers, and a check was made.

An instance of imposition, on the part of these vandals, is recounted, where a colored man, who was known to possess but one child and his wife, claimed nine children. Being told he might just as well claim a little more, and get something worth while, he nonchallantly, and without apparent effort, run his family up to fifteen members. This is one case among hundreds of a similar character.

Planters and merchants along the line of the overflowed district positively assert that they are unable to obtain labor upon their farms, plantations, and in their stores, when offering $8.00 per month and board for the same. Work is the last thing they want. When forced to it from starvation's call, they work long enough to get well filled with edibles and a few dollars in the pocket, then they jump their benefactors, and seek the cane swamps to sleep in the sun, or the orgie of the cross-roads to soak their black hides in corn juice.

It will take months to disabuse the minds of the colored people along the line of this distress, which reaches from the gulf to Cairo, Ill., in regard to free rations.

The sufferers are to be sympathized with and aided, and they are thousands ; but the vampires that invest the alluvial bottoms of this famous river, when applying for assistance, should meet with the quick desert of arrest.

AT COMMERCE STATION.

Four days and eight hours from Cairo, and we have passed the rolling country contingent to the river boundaries along the States of Kentucky and Missouri. The greatest distress imaginable was found here. Starvation and flooded households, with drowned stock, were upon every hand.

Such relief as we could command was extended and we proceeded on our way.

About five miles below Commerce, three women and two men were discovered on the third floor of their dwelling. The roof had been dismantled, the rafters and cross-beams been placed diagonally across the main structure, and the furniture, consisting of a shambling bedstead, discolored mattresses, and worn-out bed-clothing, had been pulled from the lower portions of the house onto this improvised platform. They had been in this condition for three nights and two days. The remnants of a meal, consisting of bacon rine and a few well-picked ham bones, were all the indications of food in sight. They stated that the water rose so rapidly they were unable to get out of the bottoms. In less than three hours from the first warning of the approaching flood they were surrounded by water, with an average depth of three feet, and in six hours from the time the flood struck them, they were forced to the roof of their building, and a surging sea, fifteen feet deep and apparrently ten miles wide, swept past them at the rate of 12 miles an hour. The proprietor of this establishment informed me he was the owner of 23 head of milch cows and five mules that had stampeded, some of them gaining the high ground. Pointing southward, and a little to the right of our location, I was directed to look at a clump of trees swaying beneath the force of the current. There may have been eight or ten trees in this group, none of them larger in circumference than a man's arm. Fatally lodged and entangled in their trunks were four of the cows referred to, with horns locked in the branches; several buzzards were contesting the ownership of the carcasses with flocks of crows.

Reaching the tug, in the captain's gig, which he had courteously extended to me, we proceeded to a group of cattle standing neck deep in the river just below the

O. K. LANDING.

The report at the landing was that they had been confined in that condition for thirty-six hours. Hauling alongside, they were dragged on board. These beasts were so exhausted that they fell broad-sides to the deck and lay motionless. Provender was provided and offered, and refused by all but three out of the nine rescued.

Five died before Blue Point was reached, where the living were landed and the dead carcasses were consigned to the muddy stream, to be corralled by the starving thousands south of this point, and devoured as a God-send by their captors.

The river at this point and date was estimated to be seventy-five miles in width.

BEND OF 14.

"Doc. Smith," who is in charge of this landing, had five families, in all twenty-nine persons, living in his wood-boat. These people were only half clad, and had lost everything they possessed in this world but their lives.

Squire La Duke, postmaster at

HATHAWAY'S LANDING,

was completely wrecked, escaping with his life on an improvised raft, hastily nailed together, from portions of the wharf-boat. This, I learn, was accomplished while going down stream at the rate of ten miles an hour, and half the time up to his neck in water. He was rescued fifty miles south of Hathaway's Landing.

CHAPTER VII.

"HORROR ON HORRORS HEAD."

One of the most painful sights, surrounded by the horrors of a ghastly death, it has been my lot to witness in this voyage of over 800 miles on the bosom of this flood, was encountered while coasting along the low, wood-studded shore on the Arkansas side, in company with the first mate and two deck hands of the Steamer Gold Finch. The balance of my commission were in charge of the tug at Hathaway's Landing. In turning an abrupt bend in the overflowed district the dangling bodies of a man and woman, waist deep in the water, were noticed hanging from the limb of a huge oak. The eddying current, as it rushed and swailed round the trunk of the tree, twirled and twisted these victims of the avenging flood until it seemed as if they were dancing a demonical waltz to the roar of the water.

The sight was sickening!

The starting eye-balls and protruding tongues, as they danced about through the action of the water, drove terror to the hearts of the occupants of that yawl. It was human to cut them down and give them a Christian burial, but to approach them through the gathering darkness, to clasp their dead and reeking bodies, was something the superstition of the party would not allow. We will report it, and come on the morrow. They are dead, and beyond any earthly assistance. Such were the excuses hurried through our minds, and we drifted away southward with the swelling tide.

I cannot picture to my readers the horrors of that sight.

As we left, the early moon stole in upon the scene, and bathed them in a saddened shroud of light. The waters whistled by our boat as it carried us farther away, singing a dirge to the hapless victims, who, crazed with their surroundings, ended their living horrors in strangulation.

CHAPTER VIII.

A REGION OF GLOOM AND HOPELESSNESS.

On March 9, I visited Arkansas City, Arkansas. The trip was made in a skiff, rowed by two impoverished mulatto boys about fourteen years of age. The town, at that time, was from two to ten feet under water.

In skirting the edge of the woodlands which bound the city on the west, I came across a half submerged house. Approaching an upper window, I discovered an old man, the father of the husband, who, with his wife and two children—one an infant—were crouching upon the hastily thrown together remnants of a bed. The son of the gray-haired sire, who bore the appearance and attitude of being completely broken down, remarked, upon being interrogated, in a hollow voice tremulous with exhaustion :

"We did not expect a break in the levee. The other morning we awoke, and found water surrounding the house to a depth of two feet, and rapidly rising. Before night we were driven completely from the ground floor, and took refuge here. Believing that a break in the levee had caused the overflow, and thinking that other breaks would follow, and thus more equally distribute the water, I foolishly caused my family to remain here. I fear it is our tomb."

"Had you provisions in the house?"

"No ; we have eaten nothing in the last forty-eight hours."

"Prepare at once to accompany me in this boat."

The gleam of light which shot athwart his countenance at the possibility of being delivered from his grave, will be remembered by me as long as I tread this mundane sphere.

The following day, when drifting southward with the current, a small knoll of dry land was encountered, upon which seven half-starved creatures were huddled together. The spokesman of the rescued party said : "We were unable to get out of the bottom, the flood was so sudden, and were driven on a run to this patch of dry land."

This would have afforded relief for about twenty-four hours longer. I returned within thirty-six hours over that same spot in the steamer Belle of Memphis, and the angry waters had swept it from existence.

There was in this party of seven, sitting apart and upon the water, looking off with weary eyes and saddened face, an old man, unknown to his six captive comrades.

"I guess he's gone, boss," sententiously remarked a burly negro who was busy in holding together the rags which partly covered his nakedness.

"He's been carin' on all night 'bout his darter; you speak to him, boss."

The old gentleman was lifted to his feet from his half reclining position. He was so faint from the lack of food he tottered unless supported.

"I was living with my daughter, he feebly remarked, as he gazed about the scene, with eyes filled with tears. "Have you seen her?"

"Your daughter shall be cared for; come with us."

"But I cannot find her; I have not seen her since that night the flood rushed upon us. Ah, my God, you could not have been so cruel as to take her from me!" And, burying his face in his hands, to shut out the sight of his daughter's face, as the conviction swept over him that she was drowned.

"I'll tell you how it was," he nervously added, after rallying a little.

"We did not have time to make arrangements; the water rushed upon us. I called for my daughter, my Emily, my brown thrush; for she could sing, gentlemen; ah, you shall hear her—to follow me, as I jumped from the window where we were standing. When I reached the flood the terrific current carried me away like a feather. I heard my daughter scream as she leaped after; I attempted to answer her, but I was strangled; I was borne along by the waters. Striking a tree, I seized hold of it and clung to it; lifting my head above the water I called to my daughter, but the mighty roar of that flood was the only response. Do you think she will come?"

"Yes, in the other world she will come to you.

And the old man settled again into that stolid, dreamy look, which told of a mind fast losing its hold upon the seat of reason.

CHAPTER IX.

The steam tug Flying Scud, on board of which was our special envoy, had up to this time traveled 900 miles, including its research among the bayous, sloughs and tributary streams of the Mississippi River below Cairo, Ill. The members of this expedition over the flooded country have supped their fill on horrors which shocked the stoutest hearts, and unnerved men of steel. They have passed through a country that, fourteen days prior to January 21, 1882, had bloomed with nature's early foliage, and been peopled with a thrifty, intelligent working class and wealthy planters.

And they still looked out upon a limitless sea of turbulent waters. North, south, east and west, occasionally relieved at the horizon by the budding tree-tops, there was an eddying and ceaseless flow of this muddy torrent, and the surface of the mighty river was still dotted with the carcasses of dead animals and fragments of broken buildings.

We continue to steam south. Relief is furnished three negroes, who are taken in an exhausted condition from a tree about one hundred yards from the banks of the Mississississippi. They have eaten nothing in four days.

In a feeble voice they recite the struggle they made to rescue others of their class, a half mile distant in the interior, where they said the water was four feet deep when they left, forty-eight hours before.

Becoming exhausted from their efforts, they are finally forced to abandon their humane exertions, on account of the rising water, when they embark in a dug-out and start for Point Clear, six miles distant. The frail boat is caught in the current, overturned, and they swim to the refuge from which they are taken. Twenty-four hours more, and they would have perished from exposure and hunger, and swelled the list of mortality, whose verdict is "DROWNED BY THE FLOOD."

HELENA, ARKANSAS.

A city of 2,000 inhabitants, is from two to eight feet under water.

This condition of affairs is due to the back water.

Business is paralyzed.

Boats of every description are carrying hundreds north and south to the highlands. Poultry, dogs, and household animals and pets sweep by the curbs of this once handsome city, and are hurried away to their death. Wild deer and coons have been forced into the city by the back water, and swim about the streets, giving vent to piteous wails of fright. They are clubbed to death by enterprising speculators, skinned upon the roofs of stationary buildings, and their hides sold to fur dealers, who seem to have instinctively been forewarned of the situation, and flocked to the deluged country in hundreds..

Of course the most dire distress reigns throughout this region of country. Government supplies are furnished, but there is hunger and exposure for hundreds in and about an area of this city twenty miles in extent.

CHAPTER X.

STARVATION AND DEATH.

The following special has been handed me by a staff representative of the *Times-Democrat* of New Orleans, bearing date, Memphis, March 10th, which says, of the country south of the point from which I am writing, " * * * As an example of how thousands below here are subsisting, the following instances are cited: Capt. J. Ferd. Rogers, one of the largest planters in Walnut Bend, has water from two to six feet deep all over his farm. His residence, which is known as White Hall, being one of the handsomest in the county, has water sixteen inches over the first floor. His family were brought here, but his hands, to the number of 120, remain on the place. They all live in the stable lofts, and do their cooking on the roofs of their cabins. At Charles O. Faber's place, also in Walnut Bend, the negroes there, to the number of eighty, are living on the roofs of their cabins and in the gin-house loft. They are provided with provisions from here, which are taken to them in skiffs and dug-outs. The Clayton place, Walnut Bend, owned by W. A. Gage, has about 100 negroes on it. They too are living in the gin-house and in the upper stories of their cabins. This place was considered above overflow for thirty years, and when the back water from the St. Francis River began flooding the adjacent farms, planters brought their mules to the high grounds on this farm, but the present overflow has wiped out all the marks of previous years, and the water is now two feet deep over the highest land on the farm, and all the mules of the country around were brought to Memphis to keep them from drowning. J. T. Fargason, another large planter in Walnut Bend, has 200 negroes on his place who are cooped up in the gin-house and on the top of their cabins, with water all around to the depth of four feet. J. W. Rogers has seventy-five negroes on his farm in the same neighborhood, all living in a like manner. Three were drowned yesterday by the capsizing of a dug-out. J. N. and J. W. Falls have a farm in Walnut Bend, on which there are about 125 negroes, who sleep in the upper story of the gin-house and in the stable loft. Jesse Forrest, another planter, has 100 negroes on his plantation, who are similarly situated. Frank Rogers has seventy-five negroes on his place who live in his gin-house. Bent Dupuy has seventy-five negroes, all living in stable lofts and the upper story of his gin-house. At Dillard & Coffin's place, near Delta, there are 180 negroes living in the gin-house. The cooking is done on a small strip of levee just in front, and the provisions thus cooked are taken in dug-outs to the gin-house. J. R. Jeffries, near Glendale, has 150 negroes on his farm, who are living in stable lofts and in the gin-houses. On Jacob Thompson's place, between Glendale and Delta, there are 250 negroes living on the roofs of their cabins and the gin-house and stable lofts. What is true of these is also true of every farm between Memphis and Greenville, Miss. It reminds one of so many black birds, seeing the negroes on the roofs of their cabins.

At Rosedale, the county site of Bolivar County, Miss., there are but three families remaining. W. C. P. Jones, the proprietor of the hotel, lives in the second story with his wife and two children. The water is two feet deep on the ground floor, and he makes his entrances and exits from the building by means of a dug-out, which he paddles through the main hall and half-way up the stairs leading to the second story. The water rose so suddenly in the house of Mr. Oliver Alexander, a merchant of Rosedale, that he sought shelter in the Masonic lodge-room with his wife, and luckily, too, for both his storehouses and dwellings were completely submerged. Mr. Alexander is quite sick, but is being carefully nursed by his heroic little wife, who remains with him. George P. Melchoir, sheriff of the county, also has his family with him. The water is up to the ground floor, and his residence was on the highest land in Rosedale. The other inhabitants of the place have gone and are now refugeeing in Memphis and Helena.

The country between here and Madison, on the St. Francis River, is covered with water to the depth of ten feet, and the inhabitants are living in the second stories of their dwellings. Hundreds of negroes are on the high ridges, but have no shelter, and it is a difficult matter to reach them with provisions. They subsist on the dead carcasses of cows that float in the current, and many have died of exposure. Cattle can be seen on little mounds that were built by the Indians, where they are standing in water two feet deep and hourly dying of starvation.

The extent of the great distress that now prevails will never be known, nor the loss of life that the waters have caused. Each day adds to the story of suffering, and the end is not yet."

We pass down and over the fertile and renowned

BIG CREEK BOTTOM LANDS,

south of Helena. Here, I learn that two women had been

confined—one upon a raft and the other in a gin-house, after
they had been driven from their homes by the flood, without
the slightest comfort known to the civilized world, the wind
cutting mercilessly around them. The mothers were hardly
half clad, and had no garments at all for the little ones; no
fire, no food to be had under any circumstances; the swift
current of the overflow rushing, and anxious eyes looking
for rescue from all directions in general and none in particu-
lar, the water in the meantime rising rapidly, adding to the
despair which had already wellnigh culminated. The scene
was one that pen could not describe faithfully.

These people generally lost all their personal property,
even most of their clothes that were usually worn, the water
coming so rapidly they were glad to have an opportunity to
save themselves. If they are not entitled to the aid of the
Government it would not be possible to find a single deserv-
ing object throughout the length and breadth of creation.

Supplies were issued to-day, for five days, to 1,149 people
by the sub-committee in this city.

Returning to Memphis to forward dispatches, I found
the following dispatch to Gen. Beckwith, of the Commissary
Department at St. Louis, dated Memphis, March 13, and
signed Capt. J. S. Loud:

" I have just arrived here. I found Pemiscot County, Mo.,
in a distressing condition, being almost entirely submerged,
and about 1,200 people entirely destiute. The supplies sent
to Gayoso are being carefully distributed, and will last until
about March 25. More should be sent there. The people
will be in just as bad a condition when the water goes down.
The Government, to prevent starvation, should care for them ·
at least until May 1. About fifty people are destitute at
Hathaway, 150 at Tiptonville, 200 at Hale's Point, in Tennessee, 150 at Bayfield Point, and 1,500 in the vicinity of Osceola, Ark., are destitute and badly in want. Some stores have
been received at Osceola, but they are insufficient."

And the following was received by the same gentleman from Capt. Lee, dated Memphis, Tenn. :

" I returned here on Saturday night. My dispatch of the 9th inst. falls short of representing the actual destitution and magnitude of the overflow.

" If an additional appropriation.is made, 500,000 rations of meal and meat should be sent here as soon as possible, in large instalments, for sufferers in the State of Mississippi. This is in addition to any rations that may not yet be sent from the first appropriation. Destitution is general and increasing. There are 9,000 destitute persons in Bolivar County alone. My estimate will carry the sufferers through to April 10, and possibly the flood may subside by that time, so that the sufferers can begin work."

Capt Lee was directed by Gen. Beckwith to take charge of the little steamer Anita, which left here yesterday, and proceeded at once on the mission designated for her—the picking up of parties of destitute people in the flooded districts, and taking them to dry land and shelter, where they can be comfortably cared for.

Secretary Lincoln telegraphed Gen. Beckwith that if he had not boats enough at his command more would be provided. The Secretary has also ordered the largest steamer at Little Rock to proceed at once to Memphis and report to Capt. Leland, and Capt. Lee will take the little steamer Anita, on her arrival at Memphis, and go up the Yazoo and Sunflower rivers, and distribute supplies and render what assistance he can to those in need.

CHAPTER XI.

ENTIRE CITIES SWEPT FROM EXISTENCE.

The Government has done all that is possible in the time. I have seen the Commissariats in charge of the commissary supplies at various points in the river between Memphis and Vicksburg, issuing their rations to the famished thousands

without stint or question, rather than let a genuine case of distress pass unheeded, in refusing those possibly taking advan-
tage of the situation, and imposing upon their benefactors.

Mouth of the Yazoo River.

From Vicksburg to New Orleans, a distance of 381 miles,
it can be safely stated that the country for a distance of sixty
miles in width is entirely submerged.

Austin, in the State of Mississippi, seventy miles south of Memphis, is swept from existence.

Steaming over the levees, my commission enters the city, and make soundings from the third story of the court-house, which occupies the main street of that once prosperous town. The water is found to be

TWENTY-FIVE FEET DEEP.

Houses that once had a local foundation were found half a mile distant, and the novel spectacle of entire families cooking upon rafts, the roofs of their houses, and in flatboats, was to be seen and encountered on every side.

DELTA,

opposite the city of Vicksburg, is entirely submerged. An easy sail was made through the principal streets of this town, and reports from the few inhabitants remaining to mourn the loss of their entire substance, was to the effect that the entire country for miles, in all inland directions, was flooded to the depth of from two to four feet.

Mr. J. C. Frank's large estate,

AT BLEDSOE,S LANDING.

hitherto supposed to be above any possible overflow, is flooded to the depth of two feet. Corn cribs built on a slight elevation are ten inches under water, and the stock, consisting of several hundred mules, was saved with great difficulty.

The country adjacent to, and at the junction of the

TALLAHATCHIE, SUNFLOWER, YAZOO, AND BIG AND LITTLE BLACK RIVERS,

is covered with water from three to twenty feet deep.

Hailing the steamer Dean Adams, to forward dispatches to Vicksburg, I encountered the sad spectacle of starving negroes. A colored woman, Martha Green, with two children, were refugees on the steamer Dean Adams, and was, among many others, flying from the devastation of the flood near Riverton. She was utterly destitute, and presented a sad picture, as, with tattered garments and sunken cheeks, she and her children roamed up and down the deck, not knowing what course to pursue. When the overflow first came, carrying off their little log cabin, and with it all their personal effects, the husband had gone on a boat to Memphis, as he said, to procure assistance ; but that was the last seen of him, and he has either been drowned, or has left to rid himself of his starving dependents. Some ladies, cabin passengers, took the poor creatures in hand, and provided provisions and shelter for them. The experience of this poor woman is the experience of thousands who are to-day without means of their own to support themselves for the coming few weeks, when the bottoms will again be tillable.

CHAPTER XII.

DEATH ON ALL SIDES.

Embarking again on the afternoon of March 14, we steam direct for the

YAZOO RIVER,

397 miles south. As we cast off our moorings, we enjoy the opportunity of signaling the now famous steam tug dispatch boat of the *Globe-Democrat*, St. Louis, under the directions of the brilliant correspondent of that daily, Mr Alf. H. Spink.

Norfolk, De Soto, Commerce and Austin, once thriving centres for plantation supplies, are repassed.

They are still from three to five feet under water.

The rays of that afternoon sun glittered along the rippling current of water sweeping through their streets.

There were no living indications of former life.

Several beef carcasses, and the gaunt skeleton of a favorite hunter, are seen lodged against some half dismantled outhouses, that have choked up a bend in the street.   Unpleasant odors are palpably distinguishable for a distance of ten miles along the Mississippi boundary.

There is no marked change in the river boundary of the city of Helena.

At midnight we reach

FRIAR'S POINT,

and are hailed from the shore by a signal of distress.   On landing we find the improvised raft which has been anchored at that point, floating the shrunken and already decomposed remains of

THREE WOMEN,

who had been brought in from the bottoms about noon of the day previous.

The Flying Scud being the first indications of any relief, accounted for the condition of affairs here.

If I were to state that I had positive proof that the starving wretches confined upon this flatboat, with the skeleton remains of those three women, had attempted to check famine by feeding on the corpses, would it be believed ? But I record it here as a fact.

Cannibalism, heightened by the chilling horrors of their surroundings, had been actually perpetrated on the bosom of the Mississippi River.   The bodies were consigned to the waters.

Cornmeal and bacon were left to temporarily appease their hunger.

They devoured the bacon raw.

It was with difficulty we succeeded in getting loose from the raft.   A Babylonian torrent of sound floated out upon the waters after us, as our steam whistle shrieked the prolonged signal of distress, understood by all steamers plying these waters.

At 4:30 on the morning of March 15th, we came up with a raft floating one white man and three negroes. From the white man, whose name I could not learn, came the startling intelligence that John Patterson, a well-to-do farmer, who resided with his wife and three children four miles in the interior, lost all his stock, consisting of twenty mules and about 100 head of cattle, by drowning. This so worked upon his mind, seeing the results of many years of labor swept away in a single night, that he lost his reason, and is now a raving maniac.

"Are you sure of this?" I asked.

"Well, I reckon I've worked for him befo' and since the wa'.

A member of my crew, as he afterward remarked, felt like dispatching this craven on the spot, for deserting his associates in the hour of their extremity.

"Well, Mr. James Collins, who lives at Benhaurd's Landing, says," continued my informant, "that he had occasion the other day to go near Patterson's house, and as he was passing by in his dug-out was hailed by Mrs. Patterson, who cried to him for food. She and her children had been in the upper story of their dwelling with her crazed husband for two days, without anything to eat."

Who can picture a scene more sad and sorrowful than this, and yet it is but one of hundreds that the devastating waters have wrought in their destruction of many homes that but a few short weeks ago were happy and joyous ones.

APPALLING DISTRESS.

It is authentically arrived at that counties with a population of

70,000 INHABITANTS

are submerged. Tunica County, Miss., has

5,000 STARVING AND DESTITUTE

men, women and children. The loss in stock along the line of the river, 100 miles north and south of Vicksburg, Miss., can be classed under the term, annihilation.

The carcasses of 300 dead cattle were washed ashore at Vicksburg in fourteen hours, and 413 at Greenville, Miss., in eighteen hours. A brisk trade has been inaugurated on the shores of the lower Mississippi in coralling dead cattle, skinning them, and selling their hides.

The affluvia arising from the decaying animal *floats* is discernable for hundreds of miles. What the condition will be when the torrid heat of summer sets in throughout that section of country can better be imagined than written.

Death will float in the atmosphere of this fair valley and miasmatic ailments will continue the scourges until frost again returns.

BLACK RIVER DISTRICT.

The topography of this country is peculiar to the lowest levels tributary to the immediate boundaries of the Mississippi River. The normal condition of Black River, which is little less than a stream in August, can be classed among the stagnant water courses of the country, but the rich alluvial bottom lands adjacent to the river are good for two bales of cotton to the acre on any average season.

A. E. Gottschalk & Co's commission reached the mouth of Black River March 16th.

It was a sea of water.

As far as the vision carried, nothing relieved the monotony of the wide-spreading disaster which has settled along this coast for 600 miles.

Ruin, waste and total destruction were visable at every turn of the eye.

The swollen current, for miles along its interior course, was laden with the wrecks of hundreds of housholds, —— swept away by the avenging flood.

The distress apparent along the bottom lands, on the interior of this river, was appalling. I assert, with positive knowledge of the fact, but for the timely arrival of the *Times-Democrat's* expedition, which henceforth can flank the celebrated enterprise and charitable standing of New York's famous journal in matters of meeting public distress, hundreds would have gone to their future rewards that now live to praise the life-saving hospitality of that New Orleans daily.

AN ISLAND OF SNAKES THREE FEET DEEP.

Just south of Helena, on the Arkansas side, on the morning of March 16th, we discovered what appeared to be a moving island.

Our course was directed to bear towards this phenominal appearing ridge of moving earth. When at a distance of about one-quarter of a mile, strange and confused sounds reached our ears, in effect like a series of prolonged hisses. The glass was brought to bear upon the trembling surface of the earth, when we discovered that it was one solid mass of

SNAKES,

three feet deep. They had been driven from the bottoms to this strip of elevated land, and accumulating for weeks.

Shocking as the sight was to nervous constitutions, this battle among the slimy, crawling representatives of the evil one was watched with eagerness and not without some interest. We steamed close enough to get a perfect view of the surroundings, and found that the snakes held possession of a knoll about one-eighth of a mile in length and 100 feet wide, packed to the depth of not less than three feet. They were writhing and coiling about each other in the most furious manner, and fighting to the death.

The shores along this ridge of earth were strewn with their dead, and the surface of the current south of this point was dotted thickly with the lifeless remains of adder, moccasin, water, whip and black snakes.

Many of them were fifteen feet in length and the size of a man's arm.

To have encountered anything of this kind along the banks of the Amazon, or upon the elevated mounds in the jungles of African swamps, which are subject to inundation from the sea and rivers of those countries, would have been something expected, but on the bosom of the Mississippi, upon which floats the traffic of a country ranging over a boundary hundreds of thousands of miles in extent, it was, to say the least, novel.

Upon reaching Vicksburg, Miss., now famous in civic circles as formerly in military affairs, I find that Governor Lowry is on a brief trip to Jackson, Miss.

I am indebted to the correspondent of the *Globe-Democrat* for the appended dispatch from Gov. Robert Lowry to the following gentlemen, who form a local relief committee at this point:

" JACKSON, MISS., March 17.

To Messrs. Butts, Richardson, Robbins and others, Vicksburg, Miss.:

" GENTLEMEN.—I had just received your telegram when your messenger arrived with your letters. The contents of your letters, and the information given me personally by him, advise me fully of the condition of affairs in Delta. The steamer City of Yazoo has a large capacity, and could bring out all the people, perhaps, who are in imminent danger, as well as the stock liable to be drowned. I suggest that you send this boat at once, and let her carry along every appliance that would probably relieve the people from danger of being drowned. There may be lakes and bayous where people live that a boat cannot reach, By all means, people so situated should be relieved. Have some thoughtful, true-hearted men on the boat who are familiar with the location, to send out skiffs and " dugouts," and

SAVE THE PEOPLE

that are in danger and can not help themselves. By means
of life-boats, yawls and dug-outs they can reach almost
every one who is in imminent danger of loss of life. I
suggest that no living human being be left to die, if any
trouble or expense will save his life. People first, and
then stock.

"I can not go down to-morrow, but will wait here and
receive and answer telegrams, and advise all to communi-
cate with me here at Vicksburg. I will remain at Vicksburg as long as may be neccesary, and if, after a conference with you gentlemen, I can contribute anything in the
accomplishment of what we all desire, I will go in person
to any district of the overflowed districts. I further suggest that the most trusty and thoughtful person, and the
one most familiar with the country to be visited, be placed
in command of the boat mentioned. If Commodore Par-
isot himself would go along, he would, no doubt, accom-
plish more than any one else. I feel very great solicitude
about the whole matter, and am ready to do anything in
my power to aid in giving relief. I have telegraphed Major
Hemingway to come here by rail and go on to Vicksburg,
that he may more fully understand the entire field of oper-
ations. The distress on the smaller rivers may, and I
think probably should, induce him to change his quarters
from Memphis to Vicksburg, as he would be in easy communication with the districts on the Mississippi River and
the smaller rivers. I learned from Mr. Platt that all boats
are out except the City of Yazoo, and I have in this letter
ventured an opinion as to what she should do, which, however, is subject to change or modification by you gentlemen
who are on the spot. I only repeat, in conclusion, that I
will give whatever substantial aid is in my power, and will
be in the city on Saturday morning's train.

"Very truly yours,

(Signed)   "ROBERT LOWRY."

Cats' Island, Bennett's and Luce's Landing, and Points Peter and Moore, are entirely submerged. Capt. Satterlee, of the United States army, states that it is his opinion there are

THREE THOUSAND DESTITUTE PERSONS

in Disho and Chicot Counties.

The postmaster at Good Hope lost fifteen cows and one hundred hogs.

The town of Lacona, Arkansas, and Terrence, opposite the mouth of White River, are tenantless, and have the appearance of being some distance out in the Mississippi River.

The store at Milliken's Bend, devoted to the general merchandise incident to plantation demands, was carried by the current back into the country a distance of two miles.

CHAPTER XIII.

NEARING NEW ORLEANS.

The Landry Crevasse, Ascension Parish, is sixty feet wide. A large force of laborers from adjoining plantations are endeavoring to close it. The Story Crevasse, below Baton Rouge, is regarded beyond control. It is ten feet deep and 200 feet wide. The water from this crevasse will flow into Ship Island Canal and Lake Borgue, adjoining. There is little damage except to Story's plantation, where there were 500 acres of stubble and 250 acres of plant cane. This will doubtless be almost entirely destroyed. The ends of the levee on each side of the break at Live Oak Grove Crevasse have been secured, and the belief is that the break will be closed. Small breaks in the levees between New Orleans and Baton Rouge are being closed. A number of back levees are reported broken about Lake Concordia and elsewhere.

The Secretary of the Board of State Engineers gives the following information concerning the crevasses in this State from the Arkansas line to the mouth of the river; also on the bayous. Lafourche and Atchafalaya and Ashton Crevasses have been open since 1867. They began near the upper line of Carroll Parish and extended into Arkansas, estimated length eight miles. In Madison Parish

THERE ARE CREVASSES

at Omega, Buckner, Marenza, Milliken's Bend, Delta, Beggs and Diamond Island Bend; the last named has been open since 1867. In Tensas Parish, at Woodburn, Buckner, Point Pleasant, Ship's Bayou, Hard Times, Fordfield, Hardscrabble and Kemp; in Concordia Parish, at Claremont and Glasscock; the latter has been open since 1874. In Pointe Coupe Parish, at Morganzia and Pointe Coupe, the former open since 1874. In Ascension Parish, at Landry Place. In St. John the Baptist Parish, at Bonnet Carre, open since 1874. In St. Bernard Parish, at Story plantation. In Plaquemine Parish, at Live Oak Grove. All the above are on the right bank of the Mississippi River, except Landry, Bonnet Carre and Story, these three being on the left bank. There are four crevasses on the Atchafalaya—Suttons on the left bank, in Pointe Coupe Parish; Yellow Bayou and Upper Winn Track, in Avogelles Parish, and Lower Winn Track, in Landry Parish. The three last named are on the right bank. There is also Crevasse Nine, on Bayou Lafourche.

SURPRISED IN BED BY THE FLOOD

Your commission has interviewed Mr. Wm. R. Smith, a seven-foot high specimen from the Arkansas bottom lands, who arrived down yesterday from the vicinity of Helena, Ark. He left his wife and two children at the Morgan Ferry, and learning that a relief committee was organized at the Exchange, he wandered thither and requested a

pass for his family to some point north, where he claims to
have friends. He says the levee in his vicinity broke two
weeks ago, during the night, after he had retired to bed.
He was awakened by the baby crying, and jumping up,
stepped into three feet of water that covered the floor.
The door was forced in by the flood, and a plank that
floated in was secured to serve as a bridge from the bed to
a stairway leading to the upper floor, occupied by another
family. He removed his wife and children and lay down
on the upper floor. In less than an hour the water began
coming through the floor, driving them to the roof for
refuge. They gained the roof by cutting a hole through
to the outside, and perched themselves on the ridge-pole,
for protection, all through the stormy night. An hour after
they sought the roof the water commenced lapping the
eaves, and the waves, driven high by the storm, dashed
over them, saturating them thoroughly. In the morning
the entire party was rescued by neighbors, and, after giving up all hopes of the water subsiding, Smith managed
to secure a pass to New Orleans, and arrived here without
any means of obtaining food or clothing, which the family
needed badly, as they were shivering with fever and ague
in the waiting-room of the Morgan Line. The father said
he wanted an overcoat worse than food or anything else.

CHAPTER XIV.

THE LOWER MISSISSIPPI.

FROM WASHINGTON, D. C., VIA NEW ORLEANS.

The Secretary of War has ordered 300,000 rations for
the overflowed sufferers, which are being delivered by the
Louisiana Commissioners. Fifty thousand rations have
been sent to the Atchafalaya. The rations issued for 22,000
people for fifteen days will soon be exhausted. Forty

thousand people are destitute within a radius of thirty miles.

CLASS OF DESTITUTION.

It would shock the hardened and desperate natures of the poor and destitute in the squallid quarters of any of our large cities, to experience the hardships and positive deprivation of the smallest necessities hourly undergone by the exposed and starving thousands along the banks of the Mississippi.

There is already, at this early season, a torrid heat at noon-day which blisters the sight and drives the half-crazed occupants of the floating shanties mad with desperation.

It is like floating on a sea of glass. Hunger adds its stings to the remorse arising from forlorn hopes.

The tattered rags secured in the hurried flight, upon the rush of waters, are soaked to shreds. Infants and children are comparatively naked.

All are barefooted.

The exposed parts of the bodies of the refugees, as they appear when relieved, are blistered and parboiled by long exposure.

With this physical condition of affairs we notice the indications of unsettled intellects. There is the leer and cowering of the broken minds which seem to demonstrate in their hopelessness, that anything will do if it is only dry and sheltered. They relapse into a heap of motionless bones and rags when left alone. There is also the bright and feverish glare of the hopeful, but aimless disposition, which exhausts itself in all directions without accomplishing any specific result.

Women, fainting and helpless, are taken from rafts, gin-houses and roofs of sinking homes to linger and die from the great and unbearable physical strain they have been subjected to for weeks. And this character of suffering extends along the boundry of the lower Mississippi for hundreds of miles.

BLACK RIVER.

We steam over the inlands at the junction of this river with the Mississippi, for a distance of 36 miles. The water has registered from 3 and a half to 9 feet the entire way.

Hundreds of the best cotton plantations are here submerged to an average depth of 5 feet.

Cattle, hogs and mules are piled up against trunks of trees, dozens in numbers, along this water course. Clouds of buzzards and crows hover and fight over their remains, which inocculate the atmosphere for miles with unbearable affluvia. There seemed to be nothing saved over this territory. All buildings were deserted and the stock was drowned.

The Government Commission and the tireless philanthrophy of the *Times-Democrat* of New Orleans, were upon this scene of destruction when I arrived. It was like sailing over the ocean's mighty morgue. The muddy, unreflective surface of this torrent as it passed southward, gave no indications of the hidden death and desolation vailed in its hurrying tide.

A pitiful scene of the helplessness of the wild animals which filled the forests and foot-hills of Arkansas, was witnessed on March 29th: The antlers of three deer were seen making for our boat. Upon reaching the side of the Flying Scud, the deer strove in vain to rest their fore-feet upon some solid and stationary portion of the boat. The cries sent forth by them, when their last hope had failed, were something to start the moisture of the heart. Their heaven-lighted eyes plead in dumb supplication for relief.

They were assisted aboard. After rest and feeding they became as gentle and docile as kittens.

It is estimated that at least one hundred

thousand people apply for rations. This number can not be supplied unless additional rations are received. Provisions will be shipped daily until all are supplied or stock exhausted. There being no funds at disposal, the *Times-Democrat* furnished the State Commissioner with forage for distribution, and then bought a steamer for the Commissioner's use, stocking it with corn, oats, bran and hay for sufferers. East of the Ouachita River stock is reported to be dying by the hundred. Apprehension is felt that the people will not be able to plant a crop, even if the water recedes in time, on account of loss of stock. A large amount of stock is arriving here now. The number of refugees is not very large. The situation is critical at Tallulah, and a steamer and two barges have been sent there. Goodrich Landing asks for 2,000 rations. A thorough examination of all the levees will be made. The National Cotton Planters' Association shipped the bale of cotton presented for the benefit of the overflow sufferers to St. Louis, to be sold or raffled.

Water from the Landry Crevasse is reported as encroaching on plantations in St. James Parish. Live Oak Grove Crevasse is probably closed. Breaks are reported at Hog Point; also in the old Racovrell Levee, Point Coupee Parish. The Airlee levee is not yet out of the hands of the contractor. It is expected to be almost completely destroyed. It was 14,180 feet long, and from seven to thirteen feet high. These crevasses will contribute largely to flood Bayou Mascar, Tensas, Black and Atchafalaya Rivers, until a decline of ten feet takes place in the river at Helena.

This decline is confidently expected by April 1st. There is, however, twelve days of continual wretchedness to pass—days that will be fraught with famine, despair and death.

OFFICIAL REPORTS.

The following telegrams have been received by Assistant Commissary Beckwith, from army officers on duty in the flooded districts of the South:

EAST CARROLL AND MADISON.

VICKSBURG, MISS., March 21.—Just arrived. Visited
Pilcher's Point, Providence and Milliken's Bend, La.
Found East Carroll and Madison Parishes in distressing
condition; 3,000 destitute in East Carroll, and 2,000 in
Madison. No destitution at Pilcher's except a few cases.
Have telegraphed the Secretary of War fully. Will go to
points below to the mouth of Red River by first boat.

(Signed)   LOUD, Captain 9th Cavalry.

FIVE HUNDRED THOUSAND MORE.

WASHINGTON, D. C., March 21.—To Beckwith, Assistant Commissary General, St. Louis, Mo. :—Purchase
500,000 rations for sufferers—bread and meat only—and
send 100,000 to Hemingway, Commissary for Mississippi,
at Memphis, Tenn., and 100,000 to him at Vicksburg,
Miss., for sufferers in Mississippi, and 50,000 rations to
Mangum, at Helena, for sufferers in Arkansa.

(Signed)   MACFEELY, Commissary General.

FROM THE ANITA.

TWENTY-FIVE MILES UP SUNFLOWER, MISS., STEAMER
ANITA, March 19, via Vicksburg, Miss., March 21.—To
Gen. Beckwith, Assistant Commissary General of Subsistence United States Army, St. Louis, Mo.: Since leaving
Vicksburg have been in lakes, creeks, and over plantations;
have rescued and returned over 200 people. Yawls
are now out bringing in the destitute from house tops and
gin lofts. By dark to-day will have over 200 men on some
large mounds one mile below here, and give them one
week's rations. All of them need tents for shelter.
Flood is six to eight feet deep over the entire country, and
rising seven inches a day. Large supply of tents should
be sent to Vicksburg for distribution, and rations, as stated
in my previous dispatches. Cattle drowning by hundreds,
and many on mounds will die of starvation. Mules mostly
saved.

(Signed)   J. M. LEE, Capt. U. S. A.

CENTRAL LOUISIANA.

MONROE, La,, March 22, 1882.

Gen. A. Beckwith, Assistant Commissary General, U. S.
A., St. Louis Mo. :

Arrived here last evening, after having visited Delta,
Tallulah, Delhi and Rayville. Distance traversed, seventy-
three miles—fifty-nine of the distance I came in a skiff,
over from three to eight feet of water. Country in a most
deplorable condition. The loss of stock from being
drowned and eaten to death by gnats is very great. The
people, rich and poor, need food for such stock as they
have been able to keep alive. If the water does not fall
rapidly most of the horses, mules and cattle will be lost,
as no means of transportation can be procured to move
them away. I have not been able to discover a single case
of actual suffering from hunger among the people, but
have no doubt that much destitution exists, and that it will
be general before many days. I will to-day complete my
duty, and, after reporting, leave for the mouth of Red
River, with a view of coming to St. Louis if the country
has been examined. Have met Knower here. He reports
all points on Red, Black and Ouachita Rivers up to this
place inspected and reported upon.

(Signed) S. C. VEDDER,
Lieutenant 19th Infantry.

ON THE OUACHITA.

MONROE, LA., March 22.—I have completed my report
to the Secretary of War. The following are the main facts
forwarded : About 4,000 people in the parishes along the
Black and Ouachita Rivers will need aid until May 1.
About 2,500 of the number are now supplied until April
1, 1,100 to April 10, 600 to April 5 ; balance need aid at
once. The greatest distress is found in Caldwell Parish :
least in Ouachita. The issue of meal is preferable to flour.
Loss of stock will be serious for want of forage. I do not

advise more aid in Ouachita Parish below Monroe or Caldwell, above Columbia.

KNOWER, Capt. U. S. A.

MOREHOUSE PARISH, LA.

MONROE, LA., March 22.—Examination complete of
matters connected with overflow at this place. Three hundred people will need aid in this ward of Ouachita Parish
for thirty days. In the adjoining ward of this parish 325
people ask rations for thirty days, and an issue will be
made to them at once by the State agent, from rations
already received here from the Government. That part of
Morehouse Parish in which Bastrop is situated will need
assistance for 600 people for thirty days. I leave here this
evening for the mouth of Red River, en route for Vicksburg and St. Louis.   S. C. VEDDER,

Lieutenant 19th Infantry.

The appended dispatches were forwarded by special
correspondents to various northern journals, and are here
reproduced for their authenticity. Being unable to cover
the enormous area devastated by the floods, I am obliged
to rely upon the courtesy of special couriers of the many
enterprising journals represented throughout the overflowed
districts, to all of whom I desire to express my heartiest
thanks.

[TRAVA.]

JONESBORO, CRAIGHEAD Co., ARK., March 15.
To JUDGE MANGUM, Supply Commissioner.

DEAR SIR : I would ask leave to state that at least 200
families in Craighead County are in a destitute condition
on account of the overflow. Their wants are immediate
and pressing. Supplies could be sent for distribution to

Buffalo Island, to I. N. Mangum, Mangum's Landing, and to J. F. Leslie & Co., Oldtown, for distribution on the west side of St. Francis River.

(Signed) Jacob Sharp, County Clerk.

      Jos. A. Weak, Representative.

      Hemer Parr, Attorney.

Tyronsa, Cross County, March 18.

Gen. L. H. Mangum: I take it upon myself to inform you of the condition of the people of the Blackfish section of country. I went up this morning as far as Mr. Organ's and found thirteen refugees in his gin-house in a destitute condition. They need immediate relief. They are out of everything in the way of eatables, and eat the beef that was

DROWNED IN THE OVERFLOW,

as it was their only chance. They manage to get a little corn from first one, then another, and grind it on a steel mill they have fixed up in the gin-house. There are about three hundred people, to my own knowledge, in the same fix, and they are bound to have relief from somewhere. They are entirely cut off from the Marion District. The leading men here don't seem to take any interest in them, and I take it upon myself to inform you of their condition. I let them have a barrel of meal and middling of meat out of my own to prolong life until they could get relief from somewhere. Can you not let them have five or ten barrels of meal and replace with Government provisions when an appropriation is made for them? If you can, let me know, and I will send down for it immediately. The water is falling nicely—15 inches up to date.

(Signed)   Eli Bailes.

LAKE VILLAGE, CHICOT CO., ARK., March 18.
To Gen. L. H. MANGUM.

DEAR SIR : If the General Government sends any rations out to this overflowed county, I wish you would be kind enough to direct some to Lake Village. There is

GREAT SUFFERING

among the whites and negroes. There has been some sent to Lema, but the destitute here are not relieved. Send to Vancluse Landing, and I will pay the freight for bringing it out here. The people need assistance at once. Hoping you will see to this.

(Signed)   GEO. J. KRUSE, Postmaster.

This is from Sheriff Haskins, of Mississippi County.

OSCEOLA, MISSISSIPPI CO., March 19.
To Gen. L. H. MANGUM.

DEAR SIR : Inclosed please find bills of supplies borrowed of merchants here by order of the Relief Committee ; also, letters from different parties in this county who are suffering. We have exhausted the supplies sent by you, also all that we could borrow, besides a great deal that has been given by private citizens. At the lowest estimate there are at least 300 people now in this county who are on the verge of starvation. Please send all you can possibly spare at your earliest convenience.

(Signed)   W. B. HASKINS, Sheriff.

SICKNESS, EXILE, DRUDGERY AND HUNGER.

A strip of land about a mile long and 200 yards wide, on the Arkansas side, 120 miles south of Cairo, Ill., found an anchorage for nine families, and such cattle and hogs as had been driven to this refuge, or had floated in on the bosom of the tide.

Completely exiled from the world, they watched with weary eyes their long delayed succor.

Famine had left its marks of gaunt cheeks and tottering step, and the apparent hopelessness of their condition had well nigh driven them insane. The dead bodies of three children lay exposed, starvation and scarlet fever the cause.

Several cases of pneumonia were found among the men and women. There had been in one of the families a hopeful birth, and the young mother, not yet out of danger, did not repine.

The anomoly of this strange sight was as striking as it was ambiguous.

Their suffering and exile was accepted with a resignation looked for in dumb brutes, and the relief afforded in the arrival of the United States Steamer Gen'l. Barnard, was accepted with an equally stoical indifference, and as a matter of course.

RELIEF MEASURES.

I have secured the following reply of the Secretary of War to the questions of the House of Representatives on the subject of the flood and forward same.

The Secretary of War has replied to the resolution of the House of Representatives, asking for an estimate of persons made destitute by the overflow of the Mississippi, and how long it was thought they would have to be supported, in which he states that the number of persons now receiving subsistence is about 85,000. The $100,000 appropriated sufficed to purchase 800,000 rations, and this supply was exhausted by the 20th in Arkansas, Mississippi and Louisiana, and would be in the other States affected about the 30th inst. No further demands are expected from Illinois or Kentucky, but from Missouri, Tennessee,

Arkansas and Mississippi the department has information
that the need of assistance will continue for a period vari-
ously estimated at from thirty to sixty days from date.
No information on which to base all estimates as to time
has yet been received from Louisiana, except that the character of the disaster is the same as in Mississippi and Arkansas.   A table was also submitted showing the number
of rations sent to the States overflowed, from which the
following figures are taken :

Missouri, 26,000 rations to 22,000 destitute persons.

Illinois, 36,000 rations to 20,000 destitute persons.

Kentucky, 1,500 rations to 800 destitute persons.

Tennessee, 20,000 rations to 5,000 destitute persons.

Mississippi, 250,000 rations to 30,000 destitute persons.

Arkansas, 150,000 rations to 20,000 destitute persons.

Louisiana, 216,000 rations to 25,000 destitute persons.

The Secretary of War has also ordered 300,000 rations to
be issued at New Orleans for Louisiana, 200,000 at Memphis for Mississippi, 50,000 at Helena for Arkansas, and
20,000 each at Charleston, New Madrid and Gayoso for Arkansas.   These are the first rations issued under the last
appropriation of $ 150,000.

CHAPTER XV.

A flatboat is overhauled, occupied by two negroes. They
hail from Capt. Willlis' place, and had left their families
with nothing to eat.   When asked how long they had been
out, replied that they had rowed all night, in hopes of find-
ing relief.   It was 3 p. m. when the conversation took
place.   Their course had been southerly, and at times
direct southwest, the current averaging nine miles an hour
They were, at the time hailed, over 150 miles from starving
families, and still aimlessly drifting further away.

The Willis place is situated a number of miles from the Sunflower, and entirely beyond the reach of yawls.

THREE HUNDRED LABORERS

were employed on the plantation, most of them without any means of subsistence. Their houses were submerged, and many instances of their occupants perched on the ridge-poles of their houses were noticed. These people were assisted with bacon, cornmeal, and other rations, to last a week by the Government Commission on board the steamer Anita.

Passing through this district, I had the good fortune to encounter the Anita Commission, on board of which was Mr. Stevens, representative of the *Globe-Democrat*, St. Louis. A thorough investigation had been made by this gentleman, and a report prepared for his paper, extracts from which I append :

* * * * * * * * *

" This is a white settlement of small farmers in the vicinity of Holland Landing. They reported that some of their neighbors had gotten away. They had preefrred to remain a little longer, but were almost ready to evacuate. The water was still rising, and the current had grown much stronger. The rafts swung about and tugged at their fastenings. Among the trees the water whirled and eddied, making navigation in the dug-outs dangerous. The houses built on stilts, which remained intact in the still water lower down the Sunflower and Yazoo, were found overturned floating about in the upper country. Possibly some one reading of the stock on rafts, and of the people starving, may wonder why the cattle are not killed to give the people something to eat. A glance at the animals would answer that question. They are skin and bones. The weather is very warm. Salt seems to have been entirely overlooked in the hurried flight from the houses. At nearly every stopping place an appeal was made for this article.

The animals, in their starved and feverish condition, would be unfit to eat, and the flesh would not keep twenty-four hours after slaughtering. The Taylor and Walker families were found in more than the average condition of distress. There were fourteen of them. All they had left in the world to eat was in a two-quart bucket. The men had turned this over to the women and children on the raft, and had settled down to grim endurance of hunger. A week's supply to these men was dished out by the Quartermaster's assistants with liberal measure.   *   *   *   *

Two miles up the river John Cleary, a new settler, came on board to urge immediate assistance. One of the rafts on which he had gotten his family and three or four cows was sinking. The logs had rolled out of position, and threatened to go down in eight feet of water. Cleary was the only man in a family of eight. Capt. Chapman hastily got a crew into a yawl, and for twenty minutes the Anita men worked at raft repairing. Cleary had gone into the swamp on a log, and worked in water to his arm-pits, getting out the material for the float to put his family on. When his raft was in shape it came out that the unfortunate people had been living on what little provisions they could borrow from the neighbors. They were absolutely without food when the Anita arrived. For several miles up the Sunflower, from the Cleary place, the houses were deserted.

A settlement of Irish families was found in better shape than most of the negroes. They had built rafts and had got some of their stock on them, as well as their families. Their houses had been abandoned for some days. Pat. Devinney had lost twelve head of stock and Sam. Griffin thirty-five. They had a dozen poor families, new settlers, living near them, with whom they had divided what little flour and meal was left, One of the neighbors, named Parm, had lost a boy by the overturning of a skiff. The water had risen five inches in the twenty-four hours preceding the Anita's arrival. The Irishmen

BEGGED EARNESTLY

for a few nails, being fearful their rafts would go to pieces. They were dependent on wooden pins. The settlement numbered seventy-five people. They had come in, tempted by the free use of the land for several years for the clearing of it. Some were just getting well started, and the water had swept away everything. They all thought their lives were comparatively safe on the rafts, but begged that the boat pass 'them slowly. Rations were issued to keep them a week. Thomas L. Brown, an old Union soldier, was found to be the representative man in the next settlement of a dozen families. He served in the 2d Missouri Cavalry his full time and then finished the war with the 15th Missouri Infantry.

"There are forty head of stock lying out there in the water," he said.

All of the men except Brown were away getting out logs to increase their raft room. The women and children were crowded together in a little hut built upon the floating logs. When the yawl struck the logs they shook in a suspiciously frail way. These people live in Sharkey County. Much of the previous work had been done in Sunflower and Yazoo Counties. The Brown Colony was made happy with twenty-five pounds of flonr.

Upon returning to Vicksburg, I find the following report from Capt. Lee, commander of the Anita:

The Government boat Anita arrived from her mission up the Sunflower River at 11 A. M. to-day, March 23d. Capt. Lee, her commander, reports having distributed supplies to 1,918 people during the trip, and returned with 5,254 pounds of meat, twenty-four barrels of flour, and thirteen barrels of meal, which yet remain for further distribution.

Rations were issued at the rate of 140 pounds of meat to every ten persons, upon which they are expected to subsist for two weeks. She will start during the night for St. Louis.

CHAPTER XVI.

THE ACCURSED.

At Bayou Lafourche, La., about forty miles from Lockport, therere is an abode of

FOURTEEN LEPERS.

These miserable wretches have been proscribed for years. How they live is an enigma without solution. The curse of the Almighty has settled about and upon them, upon them, until they have been thoroughly damned, and exiled from the world, The few stray dollars that find the homes of these disease-reeking people, are forever lost to the world, as commercial intercourse has been prohibited.

Their abodes are adjacent to the levee along the Mississippi River, on the Louisiana side. The flood, as if in revenge against whoever or whatever located these lepers along its shores, rose in its wrath, and attempted their total annihilation.

The picture presented to the invisible eye which beholds all things, as the deluge swept in and over them, surrounded as they were by all the horrors of a lingering death while facing the flood, would shock the sight of mortals. They fought with their teeth, and tore each other's flesh. Strangulation was preferred by some, as the receding waters demonstrate in leaving their bloated and blackened faces, grim evidences of their death. Drowning refugees, floating past the leper settlement, preferred to go down in sight of the only green earth on the bosom of the Mississippi for hundreds of miles, rather than make a footing on this raised mound of earth. Their shrieks availed nothing to the passing Commissioners, bent on deeds of charity, benevolence and succor.

They could see the day go out, in blood red sunsets, to be followed by nights of deepest gloom and despair, sinking hopes, and gradual desolation.

Who can tell what in their hearts befell? Summer with its perfume laden winds, and the balmy days of their glorious winters, would pass before their drowning eyes—in mocking procession. Anything for life would be their cry, even a double curse of their loathsome disease—only to live. They would watch for some deliverance, with that despair in hope,—which ends in death.

It is a chapter in the history of this flood. "What became of the lepers on that night of the rising of the waters?"

En route from the Crescent city north, I stopped at Memphis, Tenn., March 25th. To recapitulation the ground would be alike tedious to writer and reader. To demonstrate, however, the accuracy of the distressing facts as herein related in previous pages, I sight the following dispatch secured at the office of the Memphis *Avalanche* the day of my arrival:

An *Avalanche's* Helena (Ark.) special says the waters are falling slowly, but hunger and distress still reign. Planters and country people will be as destitute as in the earliest settlement of the State. In Laconia circle, a particularly rich and flourishing section, there is great suffering existing. The levee which broke there, built at a cost of $130,-000, was thought to be impregnable. This faith has cost a great loss of stock, for when the break came it was too late to save any considerable amount. Again, houses are being used for refuge both for cattle and human beings. In one house a whole family are living in the back part of their house while their mules quarter in the front room and on the porch. Lieuts. Satterlee and Richards left to-day to go to other points for further investigation, the former to Mississippi County, Ark., and the latter out on the Iron Mountain and Helena Railroad to Mariana, to consult with Col. Hewitt, sub-Commissioner of that district. The steamer Dick Jones, just returned from the sunk lands, reports the horrors there more and more terrible. The people were still eating drowned carcasses, and some few a little boiled corn.

A meeting held at Austin, Miss., March 25, passed the following resolutions :

Resolved, That a committee of three be appointed to proceed to Memphis immediately, to request and urge upon Col. Hemingway, the United States authorities, or any other persons disposed to aid us, the immediate necessity of relief being furnished the people of this portion of our county.

Resolved, That the amount of supplies furnished us heretofore has been entirely inadequate ; that many who are suffering have received no relief at all, and all who have received anything have been but poorly supplied.

Resolved, That unless relief is soon furnished, many will starve to death ; that they are on the verge of starvation now.

Resolved, That a little timely assistance will save from starvation many horses, mules and cattle of all descriptions which are confined upon short strips of the levee without any food at all. Many have already died, and are dying every day. Unless relief is soon furnished, all in this condition will die in a short time from starvation, and we earnestly urge and beg those who are living out of the water and have all the comforts of life around them to pity the condition of those we come to represent, and give from your bountiful store a small quantity to relieve from starvation both the human and the beast, who relies upon man for his provender.

Resolved, That newspapers which represent that aid is not needed in this overflowed district, are guilty of conduct that is inhuman in the extreme.

This points to the unerring fact, that notwithstanding the lavish outlay of public, private, and Governmental commissions, the insiduous and fatal distress raised by this flood passed all boundaries and all attempts to suppress it.

The following appeal to the American people, through the mission known as the

RED CROSS SOCIETY,

in aid of the sufferers—it being the first action taken by that body—is worthy of record:

TO THE AMERICAN PEOPLE.

WASHINGTON, March 23,—The President having signed the treaty of the Geneva Conference, and the Senate having, on the 16th inst., ratified the President's action, the American Association of the Red Cross, organized under the provisions of the said treaty, proposes at once to send its agents among the sufferers by the late floods, with a view of ameliorating their condition, so far as can be done by human aid and the means at hand will admit of. Contributions are earnestly solicited.

Remittances may be made to Hon. Chas. J. Folger, Secretary of the Treasury, Chairman of the Board of Trustees, or to his associates, Hons. Robert T. Lincoln and George B. Loring, Commissioner of Agriculture.

Contributions of wearing apparel, bedding and provisions should be addressed to "Red Cross Agent," at Memphis, Tenn., Vicksburg, Tenn., and Helena, Ark.

CLARA A. BARTON,
J. BANCROFT DAVIS,

FRED. DOUGLASS,

ALEX. Y. P. GARNETT,

MRS. OMER D. CONGER,

A. S. SOLOMONS,

MRS. S. A. MARTHA CAULFIELD,

R. D. MUSSEY.

WHAT SHALL PREVENT A RECURRENCE OF THIS DELUGE?

The wide-spreading disaster caused by the Mississippi River overflow will remain in the annals of modern history as something beyond, and in excess of any similar over-flow by this river during the nineteenth century. It is mooted by the Eastern journals that the present levee system is of little or no protection against an uprising of the waters of this character, and the New York *Commercial Bulletin* asserts that " Nature, in her might, has demonstrated the futility of resisting the floods by any such means," and that, " if anything is clearer than another," it is that " some more effective engineering contrivance than the ordinary levee system must somehow be devised." This is, to say the least, generalizing and insufficient data.

Before the system is denounced as inadequate, it must be fairly tried. It seems it was not inadequate twenty-five years ago. Of course, however, the proposition to reconstruct the decaying barricades opens the question of their value, A leading opinion in the city of St. Louis asks : " Are they worth what they cost? Is it necessary to the welfare of Arkansas, of Mississippi, or of Louisiana, to have the water kept out of the river bottoms? Would not those States be as well off if their agriculture adapted itself to periodic inundations, or, in other words, if the occupants of the bottoms moved back to the hills, and left the river free to pour out its flood-tides on either hand, fertilizing the soil and improving the country for cultivation, though rendering it uninhabitable? The notion that it would be wise to "let Nature take her course" is contrary to the practice of generations, but it is seriously advanced in some quarters, and may, perhaps, be given a hearing, though there is small prospect that it will be acted on."

Assuming that the levees are to be restored, the question arises, "Who is to foot the bills?" We have heretofore expressed the opinion that Congress will take no action in this direction. If it fail to act, the States must do the best they can. The opposition to the levees in Congress is many-sided.

There are, however, two Senators—Messrs. Garland and Jones—who have recently taken occasion to argue that the task is one for the Federal Government to undertake. Their views will not command enough support to bring Congress to act during this session, but they undoubtedly express the universal belief of the people and the States down the river. Mr. Jones says, for instance, that—

"It is impossible for any perfect system of levees to be maintained by the individual action of the different States, or of the counties or municipalities, or by the individual enterprise of different citizens. There is not sufficient capital in the South ; the property is not sufficiently valuable to bear the heavy taxation which would be necessary in order to protect it properly. We have tried it since the war, and we have again and again been overwhelmed by these devastating floods."

This is, of course, aside from the point whether Congress is authorized to appropriate money to construct levees to protect the lands.

But the friends of Congressional action put their appeal on other grounds than the protection of lands. In Mr. Garland's language, referring to the verdict of the Mississippi Commission, that :

"A levee system promotes and facilitates commerce, trade and the postal service:" "We have, by the testimony, a direct improvement of the commerce, a direct improvement of the navigation, a direct improvement of the postal service—three causes of jurisdiction that this Federal Government has, and no one else. This Government can build these levees, and has the authority. I could, if necessary, read authority after authority to substantiate the position I have taken in reference to the question of power. The Supreme Court has reiterated and repeated that doctrine time and again."

This opinion of the Arkansas Senator's may not be conclusive, but it is a forcible statement of one side of the case.

CHAPTER XVII.

PANORAMIC VIEW OF THE SITUATION.

I have no means at hand to ascertain the amount of rations or total appropriations of the Government to the distressed country. As it will require the assistance of the Government, or some other source of supplies, for at least four weeks longer, any figures at this time on the subject would be premature. While everything has been done for the distressed that could by any means be controlled and sent them, there will be found, later on, that a woful amount of unrelieved distress existed.

THE CRESCENT CITY.

The part taken by the Municipality of the city of New Orleans, and its generous, sympathetic, warm-hearted people during this carnage of destruction by the floods, stands symbolic of the many charitable deeds, public and private, that have long since been enrolled upon the escutcheon of one of the fairest cities in the country.

The marriage feast of the Carnival was scarcely cold, ere the groaning boards were stripped, and the knightly supporters of that ancient pleasure-god were fighting the rushing waters at the levee protection of the city.

All commercial and social intercourse was a matter to transform itself into wide-spreading relief and life-giving succor.

For weeks it figuratively stood waist deep in the struggling floods which fought for the total annihilation of the city. With no cessation the nights and days moved in their cycle, each in turn reflecting the horrors of that possibility total destruction. To exist under such mental and physical strains, with the attending knowledge that a commercial paralysis encircled the city, is to possess the Spartan qualities of man the days Theomopala boasted of.

As is usual in such public calamities, the half of the Crescent city's magnamity in this crisis will never be told. But its warm hearted people are stirred with the knowledge that their succor and relief went out to their own kind; that the fraternal bond of sympathy which they sent up and along the banks of that deluged country, and throughout the blossoming Valley of the Mississippi was given to those in common with themselves, indigent to the social and political structures of their country and soil.

But the mantle of relief is falling from the hands of an indulgent Providence. The waters at this time of writing are slowly but surely receeding, and the drenched earth appears in sight again.

Death lines the boundary of this, the greatest flood of the Christian Era, but its skeleton frame will soon be buried 'neath blossoming boughs and the milky cotton ball.

Contentment, prosperity and wealth will soon sing the surcease of summer, and plenty fill the land so ruthlessly laid waste by the floods.

FALL OF THE DELUGE.

The loss by the floods of the Ohio & Mississippi rivers will never be computed.

It would be next to impossible, if not entirely so, to sum up the ravages of the waters of the Mississippi as it swept down and over an estimated area of

75,000 SQUARE MILES IN EXTENT.

Habitations, out-buildings, farm-implements, cotton-gins, stock, and many lives, have gone Gulfward in the overflow.

The surface of the earth stretching south from Cairo, Ill., to the Gulf presents the sickening aspect of a vast plain swept by desolation and death.

Tons of mirery and sandy deposits have been lodged upon fields sown with the cereal grains and planted with the great staple of the South, cotton seed.

For a distance of 700 miles the shores are dotted at frequent intervals with the rotting remains of beasts, household goods, farm machinery and dwellings. The interiors back for 20 miles, on either side, along this entire distance are sad spectacles of distress and utter ruin. Forced back by the rising waters along the low bank level of the river, the refugees fought step by step until surrounded by the rushing floods they are driven to tree and house tops to be finally starved and drowned.

Days and nights of exposure have stricken thousands with paralysis, pneumonia and other lingering but deadly ailments. Indeed, the fair country of South land, along the banks of this great river, has become a vast sepulchre, for the remains of man, beast, and commerce.

The moral of this scourge, if so pleasant a view can be taken of what seems to have been aching to a curse from the Almighty, must be sought for in the apathy of a government which receives annual tithes to the amount of millions from the very spots that have, in many instances, been swept from existence, and in all instances suffered irretrievable damage.

Capital and a herculean enterprise have been lodged upon the banks of the Mississippi at the present site of the city of St. Louis, for nearly three quarters of a century. This leading commercial centre of the West annually forwards along the waterway of the Mississippi river and its tributaries hundreds of millions of dollars worth of the various products indigent to the manufacturer, planter and the vast number of mercantile institutions, stretched over a distance of 1,200 miles to the Gulf.

The importance of a centre that yearly demonstrates its commercial position in the grand congress of the world's greatest seats of commerce, should make itself felt at the doors of our national capitol when asking for protection against the oft repeated floods that lay waste her markets and paralyze her commercial life.

Upon the principle that the past has always been outlived in the success of the present and magnificient promises of the immediate future, the horrors and distress attendant upon these overflows are easily and conveniently forgotton and nothing is done.

Upon the Ohio river, which becomes a tributary of the Mississippi at Cairo, Ill., the same sad spectacle of desolation can be witnessed.

Three cities, with a total population of quite three quarters of a million, find a large per cent. of their revenues eminating from their water fronts. Their fleets number hundreds of boats, representing millions of dollars of investments. A total suppression of commerce on the river ensues during these floods. The loss incommutable.

A government that lies in wait for its tolls has left the frail supports of this transcontinental highway to the seas unguarded, to go down in the first assault of the floods. It has been accepted, as a matter of course, that ages have passed with only spasmodic recurrences of these playful features, to light up the horrors of every day calamities. Hundreds of lives and millions upon millions of property are annually exposed to these destructive overflows, and no action has as yet assumed even definite shape from which it is safe to argue anything will be done. The waters will find their normal level. The dead, such as are not destroyed by the winged carion of the air, will find a hidden resting place. The ground will blossom and bear again its fruits, and grasses and cotton, and nature will smile over the ghastly results of this Modern Deluge.

WALT. J. RAYMOND.

www.ingramcontent.com/pod-product-compliance
Lightning Source LLC
Chambersburg PA
CBHW022154020726
47496CB00008B/2711